NINJA KID 3

NINJA SWITCH!

Scholastic Press
An imprint of Scholastic Australia Pty Limited (ABN 11 000 614 577)
PO Box 579 Gosford NSW 2250
www.scholastic.com.au

Part of the Scholastic Group
Sydney • Auckland • New York • Toronto • London • Mexico City
• New Delhi • Hong Kong • Buenos Aires • Puerto Rico

First published by Scholastic Australia in 2019.
Text copyright © Anh Do, 2019.
Illustrations by Jeremy Ley, 2019.
The moral rights of Anh Do have been asserted.
The moral rights of Jeremy Ley have been asserted.

ISBN 978 1 76066 282 0

 A catalogue record for this
book is available from the
National Library of Australia

Typeset in Bizzle-Chizzle, featuring Hola Bisou and Handblock.

Printed in China by RR Donnelley.
Scholastic Australia's policy, in association with RR Donnelley, is to use
papers that are renewable and made efficiently from wood grown in
responsibly managed forests, so as to minimise its environmental footprint.

10 9 8 7 6 5 4 3 2 1   23 24 25 26 27 / 2

ANH DO

illustrated by Jeremy Ley

NiNJA KiD 3

NINJA SWITCH!

A Scholastic Press book
from Scholastic Australia

ONE

My name is **Nelson Kane**. Until I turned ten, I was a skinny, unfit

NERD.

Then on my **tenth** birthday, I woke up with :**awesome**: NINJA skills!

Now I'm the # NiNJA KiD!

But I'm still a bit of a nerd!

Don't forget
your hanky!

I got my **ninja powers** from my **dad**.

Dad **mysteriously disappeared** when
I was only little.

I live with my **mum**, Cousin **Kenny** and **Grandma** Pat on a **junkyard** in the town of **Duck Creek**.

Kenny's not just my cousin, he's my **super sidekick!**

When I become Ninja Kid, Kenny helps out by being **H-DUDE!**

He says the **H** stands for **handsome!**

KeNNy

H-DuDe!

But it should stand for **HUNGRY** because Kenny never stops eating!

Grandma is a great `inventor` but her creations don't always work the way they're supposed to.

Like the **super window-cleaning machine** that was meant to make Mum's job as a cleaner easier . . .

SuPeR WiNDoW-CLeaNiNG MaCHiNe

Or the **goggles** Grandma invented to see around corners.

Only problem was, they also made everything look **upside** ↓**down.**

It's lucky that I have such a cool family because we've had tons of **CRAZY** stuff happen in Duck Creek lately.

All the **CRAZINESS** has been caused by one man.

DR KaNe

Doctor Andrew Kane is my dad's **twin** brother. When he was young, he was very **clever**, so Grandma taught him everything she knew about inventing.

But Andrew was always **jealous** that my dad got the skills of a ninja, and he didn't. So he **ran off** with all of Grandma's inventions and became Dr Kane.

So far, Dr Kane has unleashed **GIANT MUTANT SPIDERS** on Duck Creek . . .

VRRR- EEE!

And then he created an **e-virus** that caused all the machines in town to come **TO LIFE AND** ATTACK **PEOPLE!**

With the help of Grandma and Kenny,
I was able to **shrink** the spiders back to
their normal size, and **stop** the e-virus . . .

so everything's back to normal . . .

for now.

And that's a **good** thing 'cos Kenny and I have to train for the big **athletics carnival** that's on tomorrow.

'Are you going to hang all your **GOLD MEDALS** in our room?' Kenny asked through a mouthful of banana. Even though we'd only just had breakfast, he was already eating again!

'What do you mean "all my gold medals"?' I replied.

'You're the **NiNJA KiD!** You'll win **everything!**'

'I can't suddenly win every event! Everyone still thinks I'm nerdy Nelson. They'll get suspicious.'

'They'll **never** guess that you're a NINJA!' Kenny shouted excitedly.

'Shhhhh!'

Did I mention Kenny was TERRIBLE at keeping secrets?! And his voice was really **LOUD**.

'Can't you at least win a few events?'
Kenny said. 'Otherwise Charles Brock will
win everything! Again!'

Charles Brock is the son of Mayor
Brock. He's also a **MASSIVE bully**.

DON'T wriggle,
I'm trying
to concentrate!

Charles thinks he's
the **GREATEST**
athlete Duck Creek
has ever seen.

It would be really great to win something, just once. And it would be really, **really** great to be better than Charles Brock for once, too.

Maybe Kenny was right. It couldn't be **that bad** to use my new ninja powers, just for a few events. *Could it?*

TWO

Kenny and I were at the starting line of our first practice event. It was the boys 400 metre race.

Even though Kenny was a very average **runner**, he loved to entertain everyone.

He got all the kids to start a chant before the race. Kenny even brought his own **music!**

HEY, HEY, get out of the way! 'Cos I'm in the MOOD to win and eat FOOD!

He strutted around the starting blocks. Then he did . . . **THE DAB!**

Charles was next to me on the starting blocks and tried to **psych me out.**

'Hope you like the taste of dust, Nelson,' he said. 'Because you're about to eat a **truckload** of it!'

Kenny couldn't help himself. 'Nelson could totally **thrash** you if he wanted,' he said.

Charles laughed. 'Only if it was a race to be the **world's biggest nerd!**'

Just then Sarah shouted from the side of the oval.

GOOD LUCK, NELSON!

Sarah is a girl from my class who's super smart and **super fast**. And *super nice*.

She'd just won the girls 400 metre race.

Now that I knew Sarah was watching, I desperately wanted to win. My stomach was doing **ninja flips!**

NeLSoN'S STOMaCH

Mr Fletcher **fired** the starting pistol and, without thinking, I sprinted at full speed. I'd never run so fast in my life! At the halfway mark, I was

WAAAAY AHEAD.

Charles couldn't believe it. But Kenny could! He was coming last and was **cheering** me on as he ran.

GO NELSON!!!

How's that dust tasting, Charles?!

I wanted to keep sprinting to the finish line. But I didn't want anyone getting suspicious - I'd never won a race before. Not even close!

So, with fifty metres to go, I slowed right down and let everyone **overtake** me.

As Charles ran past me, he snickered.
'Too fast, too early. Rookie mistake, **Loser!**'

Charles finished first and the new kid,
Billy Bob, finished second.

Billy Bob came from the
country and had the biggest
mullet I'd ever seen!

**Business at the front,
party at the back!**

Billy Bob was a seriously good runner. He said it was because he'd been chasing **cows** and **pigs** since he was a baby!

I finished **last** and Kenny came **second last**.

'What happened?' Kenny asked.

'I didn't want anyone guessing I was Ninja Kid,' I replied.

'No chance of that now,' Kenny said. 'Gee, I hope they don't think I'm Ninja Kid!'

'I think you're safe,' I laughed.

Sarah came over and patted me on the back. 'Good try, Nelson.'

'Good try?' Charles butted in. 'That was an epic fail! Nelson will never be a winner like you and me, Sarah.'

I wanted to tell Charles that Kenny was right. I could have **thrashed** him if I wanted to. But I **kept silent** - as silent as Kenny in a spelling contest.

Our next practice event was the high jump. Charles pushed his way to the front of the line, and cleared the bar easily on his first attempt.

I was next and just as I was about to start my jump, Charles stepped in front of me.

Just in case you DON'T know what this means . . .

It's L for LOSER!

Sarah laughed.

I knew I wasn't meant to use my ninja powers, but I massively wanted to prove to Charles and Sarah that I wasn't a **loser**. I ran hard at the high-jump bar and went

SOARING above it.

Charles couldn't believe it. Neither could Kenny!

'So much for **not** giving away your secret identity, Nelson,' he said. 'If you'd jumped any higher, you would have gone into **outer space!**'

'That was **incredible**, Nelson!' Sarah said.

Without thinking, I blurted out, 'I've been taking it easy today. Tomorrow, I'll win even **more** events.'

'Wow!' Sarah said. 'If that was you taking it easy, I can't imagine what you'll do when you're really trying!'

She rushed off to her next event and Kenny smiled at me.

'Oops, I guess now I'll have to do well tomorrow,' I mumbled.

'**Awesome!**' Kenny grinned. 'Oh . . . but I'm not sure Grandma and your mum will agree.'

THREE

That night at dinner I told Mum and Grandma what had happened at athletics practice. I was ready for them to be **REALLY mad** at me . . .

But they weren't angry, they were **worried** - which was heaps worse!

'You can't let anyone find out you're **NiNJA KiD**,' Mum said.

'Especially Dr Kane,' Grandma added. 'If he does, you'll be in grave danger.'

'No way!' Kenny said. 'The only thing in **DANGER** is Duck Creek's athletics records!'

'Dr Kane will be back,' Grandma said.
'He won't give up until he finds whatever
he's looking for in Duck Creek.'

'So, I have to come last in **everything**
tomorrow?!' I moaned.

'No . . .' Mum said.

PHEW.

'Maybe second or third last, just to be safe,' Grandma said.

WHAAAT?
Second or third last!

This was going to be the **WORST** carnival ever! I could just imagine Charles' face . . .

Maybe I should just not go to the carnival.

Then I noticed a **photo** on the fridge of my dad when he was my age.

'Wait a minute,' I said, pointing to the picture. 'How come Dad was allowed to **win** medals?'

'It was your dad's performance at that athletics carnival that made me realise he had developed the **skills of a ninja**,' Grandma replied. 'After that, he wasn't allowed to use his ninja skills when he was out of disguise.'

'I know it's hard,' Mum said, 'but you have to **trust** us.'

In bed that night I was thinking so much about the athletics carnival, I couldn't sleep.

'Kenny?' I whispered.

'Mmmmm,' Kenny groaned. I couldn't tell if he was answering me or **dreaming about food.** Most nights, Kenny dreamt that he was at an all-you-can-eat buffet **all by himself!**

m
m
m
m
m

'Kenny, I need to ask you something. My dad used his ninja skills at the athletics carnival and no-one suspected anything. Do you reckon I can win a few events tomorrow without **blowing my cover?**'

'Yes,' Kenny mumbled.

'**Really?**' I was surprised.

'Yes, I will have two slices of mud cake please!' Kenny replied.

He must have been enjoying his all-you-can-eat buffet dream!

'I'm still going to take that as a "yes",' I said. Then I **drifted off to sleep.**

FOUR

The next morning, Kenny and I got dressed for the athletics carnival. Kenny had found his outfit at the second-hand shop and he was really **PROUD** of it.

'C'mon, let's go, Kenny!' I called out, after saying bye to Mum.

'We've got to say goodbye to Grandma, too!' Kenny said.

'Alright, but **super quickly!**' I replied. 'We don't want to be late.' Kenny and I were **ALWAYS** late to school.

We found Grandma in her workshop. She was working so furiously on a new **invention** that she didn't even notice us come in.

At the same moment we entered the workshop, Grandma pressed a **big red button** to test the contraption she was working on.

Suddenly, two bright yellow

LASERS = **SHOT** out of the **MACHINE!**

The first one **hit me** before I even had time to blink.

The second laser beam
skimmed past the top of Kenny's head,
rebounded in a

BIG ZIG ZAG...

AND HIT GRANDMA!

ZAP!

Kenny ran over to us. '**WHOA!** Are you both OK?'

'Urgh, I feel like I've been **run over by a thousand elephants,**' I said.

'I've never felt **BETTER!**' Grandma said.

Then she did a **backflip!**

WHAT THE?!

'**COOL!** Is that machine a **Backflip Laser?!**' Kenny asked. 'Aim it at me, Nelson. I want to do backflips!'

'I don't think that's what it does, Kenny,' I replied, rubbing my back.

I could barely stand up, let alone do a backflip! I had **aches** and **pains** everywhere. My eyesight was all fuzzy - like it used to be when I wore glasses. And for the first time in my life, I had a craving for a *cup of tea!*

HUH?!

Grandma stretched. And then, as Kenny and I watched on in astonishment, she did a **reverse roundhouse kick!**

HI-YA!

'How did you do that?' said Kenny.

Grandma shrugged.

Then she did a **standing somersault!** Grandma was moving like . . . like . . . **LIKE A NINJA!!!**

'Uh-oh! I think I know what's happened,' she said. 'Our powers have been **switched!**'

WHAT?!!!!

NELSON

'You have to switch them back!' I exclaimed. 'It's the athletics carnival today!'

'I will, Nelson. As soon as I figure out how this happened!'

'You mean you **don't know how** to reverse the power-switching laser?!'

'**No**,' Grandma said, scratching her head. 'It was supposed to be a machine that makes clothes out of uneaten food!'

Yuck! Why would anyone want to wear pants made out of **veggie scraps!**

'What are we going to do?!' I said, panicking.

'A power-switching machine does sound like a good idea,' Grandma said. 'I'll invent that! I'll call it

THE SWITCHEROO!'

'That will take ages and we have to get to the athletics carnival - **now!**' Kenny said.

'I'll take you to the athletics carnival in my **mobile workshop**,' Grandma said. 'I can work on the **SWITCHEROO MACHINE** while you're competing and come and find you as soon as it's done.'

BEEP
BEEP

GRaNDMa'S
MoBiLe
WoRKSHoP

OPEN

GRAN

'I can't compete if I run and jump *like an old lady,* Grandma!' I cried. 'The whole school will laugh at me!'

Who are you calling an old lady?

'You'll just have to do your best,' Grandma said.

'Sounds like a plan!' Kenny said. **'Let's go!'**

FiVE

As soon as Kenny and I arrived at the athletics track, we saw someone waving at us.

I tried to focus, but it was hard to get used to Grandma's eyesight. 'Hi, Mr Fletcher,' I called.

Kenny elbowed me. 'Dude, that's SARAH!'

WHAT?! NO!

Just when I thought this day couldn't get any worse . . .

'Ha . . . um . . . only joking,' I said lamely when Sarah came over. 'Hi, Sarah. How are you?'

'I hardly slept last night, I was so excited!' she said. 'You must be **pumped**, too, Nelson. That high jump yesterday was

out of this world!'

'Yeah, I guess. But I don't think I'll be doing that again,' I shrugged.

'Don't be so modest,' Sarah said.

'He's not!' Kenny said. 'There's absolutely **NO CHANCE** Nelson will win **anything** today!'

'Thanks, Kenny,' I mumbled.

'Well, I'll be cheering you on!' Sarah said, then ran back to her friends.

'This is going to be *soooo* **embarrassing!**' I said to Kenny.

'Look on the bright side,' Kenny replied. 'You can still set records . . . they'll just be for the s-l-o-w-e-s-t times ever!'

NeW ReCoRD!

3 DAYS 6 HOURS 22 MINUTES

When it was time to start, Mayor Brock stepped up to the microphone. **'Welcome to the athletics carnival!'** he boomed. 'I'm proud to announce that this year's carnival is brought to you by **GRASSHOPPER HELICOPTERS!**'

HUH?

'Since when do school athletics carnivals have sponsors?' I whispered to Kenny. 'And it's not like kids can afford helicopters!'

'Maybe they make toy helicopters?' said Kenny. 'Or **chocolate** ones . . . Mmmmmmm, chocolate helicopters . . .'

m
m
m
m
m

Just when I thought things couldn't get any **WEIRDER**, Mayor Brock handed the microphone to someone dressed as a **GRASSHOPPER!**

'Whoooaa!' said Kenny. 'That is one huge grasshopper! I bet **he's** great at high jump!'

'On behalf of **GRASSHOPPER HELICOPTERS**, I'd like to welcome you all,' the Grasshopper said. His voice sounded strangely **familiar**. 'I have some **exciting** news,' he continued. 'The top two boys and two girls from today's carnival will be invited to the **GRASSHOPPER HELICOPTERS ATHLETICS CAMP!**'

There was **no way** I'd be invited to that camp now that I had the athletic ability of an *old lady!* But everyone else cheered. Sarah looked really :excited:.

As the Grasshopper stepped away from the microphone, I heard Mayor Brock say, 'Keep a close eye on my son. **He's the best at everything!**'

'I'll be keeping a close eye on everyone,' the Grasshopper told him.

Mayor Brock patted Charles on the back as he left the stage. 'You better **win** every event today, son, after I talked you up to that Grasshopper!'

'Don't worry, Dad,' Charles replied. 'These **losers** haven't got a chance. I'll finish with so much gold, you'll have enough to make a **GOLD STATUE** of me!'

'If Charles' **big head** gets any bigger, he'll **float** off like a balloon!'

Kenny said.

The athletics carnival started with the long jump. I tried to follow Grandma's advice and just do my best ... but my best was **horrible!**

Charles won easily.

Billy Bob came second.

Kenny came seventh.

And I came last . . .

by a **looong** way.

Next was the discus.

I CAME LAST
AGAIN!

And I came **last** in the 100, 200 and 400 metres!

I need a
lie down...

So far, I had come last in **absolutely everything!**

Kenny came second last in every event, but he didn't care. He was just **happy** he wasn't the one coming last for a change! He got so confident he would beat me, he started eating snacks mid-race!

Charles was **coming first** in everything and letting everyone know about it.

Check out these leg muscles!

But Charles wasn't always winning **fairly.** In the shot put, his dad sneakily handed him a **lighter shot put** to use.

I tried to tell Mr Fletcher but he didn't believe me. Mayor Brock made it seem like I was just **JEALOUS.**

'Poor kid has to make up stories because he's **so terrible** at everything,' he said to Mr Fletcher.

In the **long jump**, Mayor Brock insisted he measure the jumps himself. When Charles jumped, Mayor Brock added a couple of centimetres to his jump.

It was enough to make him beat Billy Bob, who should've been the real winner.

The Grasshopper didn't seem to notice Mayor Brock's cheating even though he was watching all of our events closely with his **beady eyes.**

Sarah was having a **great** athletics carnival. She won the long jump, the high jump and **broke the 100 metre record!**

Sarah's main rival was **Tiffany Jones**. Tiffany was a super-friendly girl with braces and **massive hair!** Tiffany came second in the 100 metres and won the 200 and 400 metre races.

Kenny really, **really** liked Tiffany,
but he always pretended that he didn't.
Whenever Tiffany tried to talk to him,
Kenny looked the other way!

Hi, Kenny...

During the **hurdles**, Kenny was trying so hard to act like he wasn't watching Tiffany that he **walked straight into a pole!**

But even Sarah and Tiffany cheering us on couldn't stop me running like an *old lady!*

In the 1500 metres, I had to stop for a rest in the middle of the race! I was going so **s-l-o-w-l-y** that Charles **lapped** me!

Sarah rushed over to me after I'd **eventually** crossed the finish line. 'What's wrong?' she asked. 'You're like a totally different person to yesterday.'

I wanted to tell her that I **WAS** a different person. I was now a kid trapped in an *old lady's body!* But I knew I couldn't tell her that!

'Er . . . um . . . my shoes are **too tight,**' I said, trying to come up with a good excuse. 'My . . . toenails must have grown overnight.'

My toenails grew overnight?!
Good one, Nelson . . .

It was pretty obvious that Sarah didn't believe me. 'Oh. Well, we all have off days,' she said.

I was **super relieved** when Mayor Brock announced we were stopping for **lunch**.

'What do you think the Grasshopper will have for lunch?' Kenny asked. **'A grass sandwich?'**

'You do know he's not a **real** grasshopper, Kenny?!'

'Yeah I know - wait, what? Really?'

Kenny and I headed out to Grandma's mobile workshop, which was parked in the carpark. 'Hopefully Grandma's invented the **SWITCHEROO MACHINE** so I can win some races after lunch!' I said to Kenny.

'Did you say **lunch?!**' Kenny replied. 'Coming second last in everything has made me **super hungry!**'

SiX

When we arrived at Grandma's workshop, I expected to see her putting the final touches on the **SWITCHEROO MACHINE**. But, instead, she was throwing **paint lids** like **ninja stars** at a target.

PiNG!

'Have you already finished the **SWITCHEROO MACHINE?**' I asked.

'Haven't started it!' Grandma replied. 'Turns out I've lost my ability to invent things!'

WHAAAAT?!

'Hang on,' Kenny said. 'If the laser has **switched** your powers, then Nelson should have the ability to invent now!'

'Good thinking, Kenny!' Grandma said. 'Over to you, Nelson.'

I quickly sat down at Grandma's workbench. 'Any idea where I should start, Grandma?' I asked.

'Absolutely none!' she said.

Then Grandma threw a paint lid at an apple

WHOOSH! SLicE!

. . . and started eating it!

'This is **CRAZY**, Grandma. I'm not an **inventor**,' I said.

'I'm not a ninja, Nelson. But look . . .'

She did a **sideflip** while eating the apple!

Flip!

'Banish any **doubts** from your mind,' Grandma said. 'And put complete trust in your ideas.'

She hadn't lost her wisdom in **THE SWITCH!**

I tried to **clear my mind** and concentrate.

Suddenly, I knew just what to do! The ideas were **flooding** into my head. Grandma's brain was **incredible!**

'Kenny, pass me a pencil and paper!' I said.

'No can do!' Kenny replied.

'What? Why?!!'

'Being an inventor's assistant is hungry work!' Kenny said. 'And I haven't had lunch!'

I couldn't believe it. 'You're too hungry to **pass me a pencil?!'**

Kenny nodded.

'Fine,' I said. 'Let's grab some lunch first. Then we'll work.'

So we all headed to the canteen. Grandma even did a **ninja roll** out the workshop door!

There was a **HUUUGE** queue at the canteen. Everyone was really hungry after the morning of athletics.

'**Hurry up!**' Charles shouted loudly to a canteen lady just as she was pulling a huge tray of **sausage rolls** out of the oven. His shout made her jump.

The tray of sausage rolls

flew high into the air...

Just as the sausage rolls were about to **Spill** to the ground, Grandma did a **ninja swipe . . .** and caught the tray on her leg! Not one sausage roll was lost!

SWiPE!

Everyone in line **cheered.**

Kenny **LOUDEST** of all.

The canteen lady was so grateful that she gave Grandma **three JUMBO sausage rolls** for free!

'I could get used to this treatment!' Grandma beamed.

'**Me too!**' Kenny agreed with a mouth full of sausage roll.

On our way back to the mobile workshop, Grandma was **skipping** ahead faster than we could keep up! She was going so fast that she didn't see she was about to **crash** straight into two guys carrying a huge athletics BANNER!

FINISH

'Watch out, Grandma!' I cried.

But instead of **crashing** into the banner, Grandma just did a **triple somersault** right over the top of it! And didn't even drop her sausage roll!

'**Rock and roll, Grandma!**' Kenny cheered.

Back in the workshop, I worked furiously on the **SWITCHEROO MACHINE** all the way through lunch. I couldn't believe how quickly my brain was working! Figuring out what went where was easy . . .

OOPS!

most of the time.

And Kenny was a great inventor's assistant, now that his tummy had stopped **rumbling!**

Eventually, I had a machine we could try.

'How does it work?' Grandma asked.

'Well . . . first, the machine captures an image of someone or something -'

'So we just invented a **fancy camera?**' Kenny interrupted.

'No,' I replied. 'The machine doesn't just take a photo, it captures something's **essence!'**

BaNaNa

ZAP!

'And then you capture the essence of someone or something else . . .'

'Then you press this button and . . .

their essence is **switched!**'

'Wow!' Grandma said. 'I'm impressed.'

'Don't be impressed until we check if it actually works!' I replied. 'Can you please pass me the banana, Kenny?'

CATCH!

Even though the catch was an easy one, without any of my ninja skills I dropped the banana. But instead of **splatting** on the ground, the banana **bounced** like a tennis ball!

BOING!

'You've done it!' Kenny said.

'Not so fast,' I said. 'Now we need to test the tennis ball.'

'I'll do the honours!' Kenny said, picking the ball up.

Kenny started to **peel** the tennis ball . . .

JUST LIKE A BANANA!

'If this really worked, then the tennis ball should **taste** like a banana!' Grandma said.

'Could this day get any **weirder?!**' Kenny asked. Then he **bit** into the tennis ball . . .

Kenny's face **scrunched up** so tight his lips, nose and eyes all met in the middle!

BLURGH!

'I'm sorry, Nelson,' Grandma said. 'You've got some more work to do.'

I was about to get back to tinkering when Mr Fletcher made an announcement over the **loudspeakers.**

Lunch break is now **over.**
Return to the track for the second half of the carnival!
Anyone not back in **two minutes** will spend the rest of the week in the Principal's office!

OH NO! I really wanted to get this machine working, and get my **ninja powers** back, before the carnival was over. I'd never win an event now.

'You better go, boys,' Grandma said.
'Don't worry, I'll **guard the machine**
until you get back.'

SEVEN

The second half of the carnival was just like the first. Kenny and I came second last and **last in every event!**

Sarah and Tiffany were still **neck and neck** in most events . . .

And Billy Bob would have beaten
Charles in some events . . .

if Mayor Brock wasn't helping Charles
cheat nearly **every time!**

The last event of the day for the boys was the high jump. Sarah and Tiffany were watching us as they waited to compete in the discus.

It seemed like a lifetime ago that I went so high over the high-jump bar that I **high-fived** a seagull.

This time, I went straight **under** the bar! My jump was **so bad**, I didn't even get **high** enough to go over the mat!

SPLAT!

Billy Bob did a brilliant jump and was leading the event with only one jumper to go... **Charles Brock**.

When it was his turn, Charles told Mr Fletcher he'd like the bar raised TEN centimetres.

Everyone was shocked. No-one had ever jumped that high.

Mayor Brock pushed Mr Fletcher out of the way. 'I'll raise the bar!' he said.

It took a while, but eventually Mayor Brock set the bar to the **record height.**

Charles ran hard and fast at the high-jump bar. He jumped really high, but it wasn't enough. His foot **clipped** the bar on his way over . . .

The weird thing was, the bar didn't fall off. **It didn't even move!**

Charles stood up and raised his fists to the sky.

YES! New record! I am the GREATEST!

Everyone moved over to the podium for the **presentation ceremony** but Kenny and I hung back to investigate . . .

The bar was **GLUED on!**

'Mayor Brock must have done it while he was adjusting the bar!' I said.

'**Hey, everyone!** The bar was **glued** on!' Kenny yelled out. 'Billy Bob should've won!'

But Mayor Brock and the
GRASSHOPPER were already at
the microphone, ready to start the
presentation, and no-one
was paying attention.

'C'mon, Kenny,' I said, and we joined
the others in front of the podium.

'I told you my son was **the best**,' Mayor
Brock was saying to the Grasshopper.

'He's definitely going to the athletics camp, isn't he?'

'You'll find out soon enough,' the Grasshopper replied.

'But I want to know **now!**' Mayor Brock demanded.

The Grasshopper spoke into the microphone. 'Alright, let's HOP straight to the medal presentation,' he said, and everyone laughed.

The Grasshopper seemed in a real *hurry*. He spoke very quickly as he made the presentations. 'The top two boy athletes are **Charles Brock** and **Billy Bob.**'

'Yes, I knew it!' Mayor Brock **jumped** up and down like a toddler at an ice-cream shop.

All the kids cheered. Mostly for Billy Bob who was doing a heel-and-toe shuffle on his way up to the podium!

The Grasshopper handed Charles and Billy Bob their **GOLD MEDALS.**

'Hey, these are just **chocolate!**'
Charles said angrily.

'Yum!' Billy Bob said.

'Just to clarify, Charles was the **VERY top boy!**' Mayor Brock added. Then he tried to start a chant.

Charles, Number One!

Charles, Number One!

No-one joined in.

The Grasshopper continued rushing through the presentation. 'The **top two** girls are Tiffany Jones and Sarah Harris.'

Sarah and Tiffany both **beamed** with pride.

Without thinking, Kenny blurted out,
'Woohoo! Go Tiffany!'
Then he tried to act like it wasn't him who said it!

Sarah and Tiffany shook the Grasshopper's hand and received their chocolate medals. They then went and stood with Charles and Billy Bob. Lots of parents were snapping photos on their phones.

'Let's get an official photo of our four **little champions** with our wonderful sponsor!' Mayor Brock said, looking around.

But the grasshopper suit lay **abandoned** on the ground.

Mayor Brock was **shocked**. But not as shocked as Kenny.

'What?! He's not a real grasshopper?!'

'I've been trying to tell you that all day, Kenny!' I said.

'Looks like we're doing the photo without our sponsor!' Mayor Brock said.

Just as Mayor Brock was about to take the photo, a massive **helicopter** flew overhead. A ¦HUGE CAGE¦ dropped down from underneath and **scooped up** Sarah, Tiffany, Charles and Billy Bob!

'Well, this is a weird photo shoot!' Kenny said.

'I don't think this was meant to happen, Kenny!' I was **super WORRIED** now.

Charles, Billy Bob, Tiffany and Sarah were **screaming** from the cage as it hung below the helicopter.

AAARGH!

The helicopter pilot yelled through a megaphone, 'One of you four kids must be the **NiNJA KiD**, and now I have you captured! You won't get in my way again!'

HAHAHA!!!!!!

I knew the Grasshopper sounded familiar! 'That's **Dr Kane!**' I said to Kenny.

I had to do something and **Fast.** Problem was, I didn't have my **ninja powers ...**

But Grandma did!

'Kenny, I'll distract Kane, you go and get Grandma!'

'**Done!**' Kenny said, running off to Grandma's mobile workshop.

Dr Kane was about to fly away with Sarah and the others. I had to do something!

I grabbed a **shot put** off the track and hurled it as hard as I could towards the helicopter . . .

but it dropped right in front of me!

Dr Kane laughed from the helicopter.

'At least I know you're not the ninja!'

'No, I am!' Grandma did a **triple-flip**

and landed right beside me.

'Go, **Ninja Grandma!**' I said.

'I'll tell you a secret, Nelson,' Grandma whispered. **'I'm terrified!'**

'You always tell us to believe in ourselves,' I said. 'Now it's your turn.'

'I see my wisdom switched over to you, too!' Grandma chuckled. She turned to Kenny. 'Alright, **H-DUDE**, let's save those kids.'

'Yeah! Let's go! That grasshopper guy is really **bugging me!'** Kenny replied.

WH

Kenny used to hate flying with the jetpack, but ever since Grandma had been teaching him how to use it by throwing food into the air, Kenny had become an expert!

Grandma and Kenny **soared** into the sky.

OOSH!

Dr Kane laughed when he saw Grandma and H-Dude flying past with their solar-powered jetpacks. 'Ninja Grandma?! Ha!'

'And **H-DUDE!**' Kenny chimed in.

Dr Kane laughed at Grandma. 'Oooooh! What are you going to do? *Knit me a cardigan?*'

HAHAHAHAHA!

Grandma plucked a paint lid from her jetpack and **threw it** just above his head!

FLiNG!

YEAH!

Dr Kane stopped laughing.

All the kids watching on below cheered!
So did their parents!

But it was the **grandparents** that cheered the loudest!

♡ Grandma suddenly had lots of new **admirers!** ♡
♡

'I love you, Ninja Grandma!'

Sarah's granddad called out.

Grandma did a **somersault** in the air.
'Release the kids!' she yelled at Dr Kane.

Dr Kane looked closely at Grandma. 'Do I know you from somewhere?' 'Only from your **WORST NIGHTMARES!**' Grandma replied. She started flinging **sets of false teeth** at Dr Kane.

FLiNG!

CHOMP!

While Dr Kane was fending off the false teeth, I saw Kenny **fly** around to the other side of the helicopter, slide in and grab the **controls**.

Kenny started **steering** the helicopter back to the ground. But Dr Kane saw what he was up to.

'Not so fast, H for Hopeless Dude,' he sneered. Dr Kane hit the passenger **EJECT** button and Kenny went **flying out.**

Dr Kane regained control of the helicopter and steered it higher. Sarah and the others were really **panicking** in the cage. Charles was shrieking the LOUDEST.

SAVE ME FIRST!

Grandma was **FURIOUS**. 'No-one ejects H-Dude!' she yelled.

Grandma **whipped** out a cup and saucer. She yanked the teabag out of the cup and started **twirling it** over her head.

She let the teabag go and it flew through the air with awesome speed.

The soggy teabag hit Dr Kane right between the eyes.

'Owww! That's HOT!'

Now Dr Kane looked really mad. He pushed a button on the controls and a **giant hand sprung out** the side of the helicopter. It **flicked** Grandma away like she was a pesky blowfly.

FLICK!

Grandma managed to regain control and land softly on the athletics track.

We needed a new plan.

'Keep Kane distracted!' I shouted to Kenny. 'Grandma and I will be back soon!'

'Roger that!' Kenny said, flying closer to Dr Kane.

HEY! Over here, KANE TOAD!

When we got back to the mobile workshop, I didn't have time to think. I just ran over to the **SWITCHEROO MACHINE**.

'OK!' I announced. 'Let's give it a try!'

'But you haven't finished the machine, Nelson!' Grandma said. 'Remember what happened to the tennis ball!'

'I know, Grandma,' I said, 'but we don't have a choice. I trust your inventing powers!'

Grandma nodded. 'I'll miss feeling this young,' she said. 'But I can't wait to have my own skills back!'

'Here we go, Grandma. **Three . . .**

two . . .

ONE!'

ZApPiTTY

ZiP

ZAP!!

At first, it seemed like nothing had changed. Then, suddenly, I felt more like my old self again. All my **aches** and **pains** had disappeared. My eyesight was crystal :clear: again!

I didn't feel **completely** the same as my old self . . . something **wasn't quite right,** and I couldn't put my finger on it. But I didn't have time to worry about that now! I looked over at Grandma.

I've already got three ideas for new inventions!

Grandma smiled and handed me my disguise and the jetpack. 'Go get 'em, Ninja Kid.'

I threw them on, hurried out of the trailer, and **soared** into the air.

Kenny was doing a great job keeping Dr Kane distracted!

'What did the 0 say to the 8?' Kenny asked.

'I don't care!' Dr Kane replied.

Nice belt!

When I joined Kenny in the sky, Dr Kane couldn't believe his eyes.

He looked down at Sarah, Tiffany, Billy Bob and Charles, still in the cage. 'Wait, I thought one of you had to be Ninja Kid!'

'No,' Sarah replied.

'That's **NiNJA KiD!**'

'And that's **H-DUDE!**' Tiffany called. 'The H stands for *handsome!*' Kenny **blushed** big time!

'Correction,' Dr Kane said. 'That **was** H-Dude and Ninja Kid!'

The **GIANT MECHANICAL HAND** burst out of the side of the chopper and tried to grab us.

We managed to **weave** out of the way, just in time.

'Hey, Ninja Kid, what can I do to help?' Sarah asked.

I came up with a plan. 'Huddle together in the back left corner and hold on tightly to the cage,' I replied.

'Nup, I'm not huddling in a corner,' Charles yelled. 'I'm not scared.'

But his legs were **shaking** like jelly.

'Moving into the corner will tip the cage on an angle,' I said.

'Yeah, haven't you learnt anything from maths class?!' Kenny added.

'H-Dude, I need you to head down and tell everyone to lay all the **high-jump** mats on the track directly beneath us.'

Kenny **flew back down**

to the ground.

I positioned myself right next to the cage. 'Is this the best you can do, Dr Kane? Or do you need A HAND?' I said.

Dr Kane steered his helicopter closer. The giant hand formed a **fist** and swung at me . . .

I weaved out of the way just in time.
The giant hand collided with the cage,
punching a huge hole in its side. Just
like I'd planned!

'Now jump!' I yelled to Sarah and
the others.

'Don't need to ask me twice!' Sarah said.

It was a big drop but Grandma, Kenny and the rest of the kids had created such good cushioning with the high-jump mats that Sarah landed like a **feather!**

Billy Bob and Tiffany jumped next.

YEE-HAH!

They landed safely on the mats, too. Tiffany ran over to Kenny. 'Thanks so much, H-Dude!' She gave him a huge **hug** and a **kiss** on the cheek!

Kenny's whole face went **SUPER RED!**

Everything was going to plan . . . except that Charles was refusing to leave the cage!

'I'm not jumping!' he said. 'I'm **SCARED**, Ninja Kid.'

'That's totally cool,' I said. 'I get scared all the time.'

'**No way!** Ninja Kid doesn't get scared!'

'Yeah, I do,' I replied. 'But I've learnt that you can **push through it**.'

Dr Kane's hand formed a **giant FIST** again. It pulled back and then started coming straight for us.

'**Jump!**' I yelled to Charles. '**NOW!**'

EiGHT

Charles landed safely on the mats and joined the others. We had done it! Everyone was safe. But Dr Kane still had a few tricks up his sleeve for me.

'Hey, Ninja Kid, you'll love this one!' he shouted.

The giant hand **karate chopped** me so hard I saw stars!

CHOP!

I knew the next time that **giant hand** hit me, I'd be knocked out of the sky. I had to change tactics, **fast.**

I remembered how I slowed down Dr Kane's helicopter last time, by blocking the exhaust pipe with an apple. I didn't have an apple . . . but I did have a **banana tennis ball!**

I lined up the exhaust pipe and threw the tennis ball straight at it . . .

SMACK!

'No new tricks, Ninja Kid?' Dr Kane chuckled. 'That's a shame. Because I've got loads more!'

Then a **SECOND giant hand** appeared from the other side of the helicopter.

The first hand grabbed me while the other hand ripped off my jetpack. The giant hands began to throw me back and forth **like I was the tennis ball!**

What was I going to do now?!

I was high up in the air with no jetpack - in any moment it was going to be **game, set, match!**

Then I had one last idea.

'H-Dude, get the **SWITCHEROO MACHINE!**' I yelled down to Kenny.

'Can do!' Kenny replied. 'Hang in there, Ninja Kid!'

'You deserve a round of applause for being such a **good sport**, Ninja Kid!' Dr Kane said.

The giant hands began to clap, squashing me into a Ninja Kid sandwich!

I was holding on by the very tips of my fingers. The hands were waving me around **wildly**. Just when I felt I was about to fall, Kenny returned with the SWITCHEROO MACHINE.

'What do you want me to **ZAP**, Ninja Kid?' he yelled up at me.

I scanned the ground . . . and saw . . .

A CHIPMUNK!
YES!

'The chipmunk!' I yelled back. Kenny lined up Dr Kane and then the chipmunk. He fired the **SWITCHEROO MACHINE**!

Dr Kane looked exactly the same.

'Did it work?' Kenny asked.

'Don't think so!' I called back.

I had **no idea** what to do next!

Then all of a sudden the helicopter lurched to the right. Then to the left. The giant hands began **twirling** around and around in the sky. One hand even gave a thumbs up!

WHOOOAAA!

I leaned around to look inside the helicopter again. Dr Kane was crouched down, **gnashing his teeth** and **chewing** at the helicopter controls!

'Actually, H-Dude, I think it did work!'

The helicopter **dived** towards the ground. When it got close enough, I jumped off the tail and landed safely on the mats.

At the same time, the chipmunk **scurried up** a tall tree and did a diving leap into the chopper! It pushed Dr Kane out of the way and took hold of the controls.

You'll pay for this, Ninja Kid! You won't keep me from getting what I want!

Weird how a chipmunk could look so **cute** but so EVIL at the same time! Next to him, Dr Kane was sitting there scratching his armpits!

The chipmunk steered the helicopter away and all the kids CHEERED.

WHUP!
WHUP!
WHUP!

Sarah rushed over to me. 'You saved us again, Ninja Kid! Thank you!'

'I couldn't have done it without your help, Sarah.'

'Hey, how do you know my name?' she asked.

Oops!

'Oh . . . ah, I heard someone calling it out,' I said.

'Oh, OK!' Sarah smiled.

Phew!

'I want to give you something,' Sarah said. She put her chocolate medal around my neck!

Tiffany gave her medal to Kenny. 'You're the coolest, H-Dude!' she said. **Kenny went bright red!**

Then he said, 'Actually, there's this guy in your class who's really cool. His name is Kenny and he's really handso-'

ARGH!

Kenny didn't want to leave, but I had to stop him from **blurting out** our secret. And we had to get changed out of our **superhero costumes** before our classmates realised we were missing!

Bye Tiffany!

Bye Sarah!

NiNE

When we arrived home, the first thing Mum noticed were the **MEDALS** around our necks.

'Nelson, you weren't supposed **to win** any events!' she said.

'Don't worry,' Kenny said. 'They're **not real!**'

m
m
m
m
m

'And it's not **my** medal, I came **LAST in everything!**' I said proudly. It felt strange to be so happy about coming last!

'I came second last in everything,' Kenny added.

And I won a lot of hearts!

As we had afternoon tea, we told Mum all about our day - about the **GRASSHOPPER**, and the **SWITCHEROO MACHINE** and defeating Dr Kane.

I looked at the chocolate medal Sarah gave me, then I looked at the **photo** of my dad with all the MEDALS around his neck. Mum noticed me staring.

'One day, Mum, I'd like to know what happened to Dad.'

'Me too,' Mum replied. 'Until then, what I do know is that if he were here, he'd be **so proud of you.**'

Mum gave me a massive hug and I gave her half my chocolate medal.

'I'm just so glad to have you and Grandma back safely,' Mum said. 'And back to **normal!**'

'Me too. Although . . . I'm not sure the **SWITCHEROO MACHINE** turned us *completely* back to normal again . . .' I admitted.

Mum looked worried. 'Really? Why not?' she asked.

'Well, I don't think Grandma used to be able **to do** **THAT!'**

READ THEM ALL!

NINJA KID 13 COMING SOON!